Rockets

CROOK CATCHERS

The Sandwich Scam

Karen Wallace & Judy Brown

A & C Black • London

Rockets

CROOK CATCHERS

Karen Wallace & Judy Brown

The Stuff-it-in Specials
The Minestrone Mob
The Sandwich Scam
The Peanut Prankster

First paperback edition 2000
First published 1999 in hardback by
A & C Black (Publishers) Ltd
35 Bedford Row, London WC1R 4JH

Text copyright © 1999 Karen Wallace
Illustrations copyright © 1999 Judy Brown

ISBN 0-7136-5128-8

A CIP catalogue record for this book is available
from the British Library.

Printed and bound by G. Z. Printek, Bilbao, Spain.

Chapter One

Lettuce Leef and Nimble Charlie were
Crook Catchers to the Queen.
It was hard work! Sometimes, even
Crook Catchers need a holiday.

At that moment, the telephone rang.
It was connected directly to the
Queen's palace!

Splatter was the Queen's trusty servant.
If there was trouble at the Palace, he
was always the first to know.

5

Before Splatter could reply, there was a
huge crash followed by a terrible bellow.

The line went dead.

Lettuce Leef put down the phone.
'There's trouble at the Palace,' she cried.

Nimble Charlie closed the office door
and turned over the sign.

Chapter Two

Lettuce Leef and Nimble Charlie couldn't believe their eyes! Usually the street up to the Palace was spotlessly clean.

Usually the flower beds on either side were beautiful and tidy.

Not any more!
There was bread all over the street!

There was bread all over the flower beds!

The Palace doors swung open before Lettuce Leef and Nimble Charlie could knock. Splatter stood in front of them. He was covered from head to toe in sandwich fillings.

roast beef and mustard

chopped egg and watercress

cheese and pickle

tunafish mayonnaise

Lettuce Leef reached for her handkerchief.

Then she stopped. Splatter needed a car wash not a handkerchief.

Suddenly the Queen thundered into the room. 'Our Garden Party is ruined!' she roared.

She threw a crumpled letter on the floor.

Lettuce Leef picked it up.

O.H.M.S

Dear yer Queenship,

No-one wants to come to your Garden Party unless you make Inside Outside Sandwiches.

They're the best.

Signed your servant

The Prime Minister.

P.S. I know you're the greatest really.

An extraordinary noise filled the room. The Queen was blubbing like a water buffalo.

'Let's make a nice cup of tea,' said Lettuce Leef.

Chapter Three

Twenty minutes later, the Queen was on her third mug of tea and everyone was feeling better.

There were two sorts of sandwiches in front of them. One was the old-fashioned kind that the Queen always had at her garden parties.

little triangles

thin slices of bread

crusts cut off

The other kind of sandwich was
totally different. It was an
Inside Outside Sandwich.

Splatter looked nervously at the Queen.

He picked up a sandwich, slurped up the filling and threw the bread on the floor.

'Do you have any idea who makes these sandwiches, Your Majesty?' asked Nimble Charlie.

'I have my suspicions!' snarled the Queen.

Splatter trembled.

'Why don't you order them
to stop making these
Inside Outside Sandwiches?'
asked Nimble Charlie.

The Queen stamped her foot and went
purple in the face.

WE HAVE TO FIND
THEM FIRST!

WE ARE
THE
GREATEST

Lettuce Leef thought about the prime minister's letter. It would be terrible if nobody came to the Queen's Garden Party.

Suddenly Lettuce Leef thought of a plan! She whispered it to Nimble Charlie.

Chapter Four

Lettuce Leef took a deep breath.

23

The Queen stuffed the last chocolate biscuit in her mouth.

'Because no one can resist showing off,' said Lettuce Leef.

The Queen's eyes lit up.

Lettuce Leef rolled her eyes. Not even the Queen could resist showing off.

Lettuce Leef headed for the door.

Chapter Five

The next morning, all the newspapers had the same front page. Down in Old Ma Sludge's kitchen one of them was pinned to the wall.

Old Ma Sludge squished bananas and brown sugar on to two thick slices of bread.

'Yeah!' sneered Bitsa Sludge.

'What's the prize?' asked Old Ma Sludge.

Old Ma Sludge upturned a jar of mayonnaise and a whole tin of tunafish on to two pieces of bread.

'She'll have to give us back our jobs!' she shrieked.

The next morning, a huge banner hung over the Palace garden gate.

Everywhere there were long tables piled with different kinds of sandwiches.

At every table hundreds of people stood about and stuffed themselves.

But at one table there were more people than at all the other tables put together!

It was Old Ma Sludge's table. She and Bitsa were handing out Inside Outside Sandwiches faster than popping popcorn!

And all around, you could hardly see
a blade of grass or a flower petal.
Everything was covered in bits of bread!

It was time for part two of the plan.
'Are you ready?' whispered Lettuce Leef
to the prime minister, who was stuffing
his mouth with an Inside Outside
Sandwich.

Rwaeddthy.

Chapter Six

There was a roll of drums and Lettuce Leef led the prime minister on to the stage.

The Queen sat in the middle on a big gold throne. Beside her stood Splatter.

Behind them both was a large white screen.

The Queen prodded the prime minister with her long purple stick.

He bit into two slices of thick
white bread covered with
his favourite filling.

A huge cheer went up from the crowd.

'Pleased to see us?' cried Old Ma Sludge as she and Bitsa clambered on to the stage and bowed.

The prime minister held up
his hand for silence.

It didn't matter that it wasn't dark.
Everyone could see the pictures on
the screen.

Bread...

More bread...

Even more bread...

'Ladies and gentlemen,'
bellowed the Queen.

For a moment nobody spoke.
Then a low grumbling started.

The grumbling grew into a loud roar.

Old Ma Sludge and Bitsa tried to run for it but the Crook Catchers were ready.

Quick as a flash, they tied them together with the Queen's apron strings.

A cunning grin spread across the
Queen's face.

Old Ma Sludge's prize
was a litter picker
with a special end
to pick up bread.

Bitsa's prize was a
year's supply of
bin bags and
an extra-strong
dustpan and brush.

The Queen stamped her foot.

The crowd parted as Old Ma Sludge and
Bitsa began to pick up the bits of bread.

It was going to be a long, hard, nasty job.

The Queen popped a dainty finger roll into her mouth.

Back at the pumpkin office there was an enormous parcel sitting on the doorstep.

Lettuce Leef read the label.

Present from the Queen
Open Carefully

Lettuce Leef gasped! Inside was a picnic basket and two tickets to Disneyland.

The End